Summer Stinks

"An alphabetical lexicon for the estivally dispirited."

by

Marty Kelley

Zino Press

CHILDREN'S BOOKS

Madison, Wisconsin

For my beautiful daughter, Victoria Rose.
You are sweeter than any summer flower.

SUMMER STINKS is published by Zino Press Children's Books, PO Box 52, Madison, Wisconsin 53701. Contents copyright © 2001 by Marty Kelley. All rights reserved. No parts of this book may be reproduced in any way, except for brief excerpts for review purposes, without the express written permission of Zino Press Children's Books. Printed in U.S.A.

The paintings in this book were done in watercolor on Arches paper. The text was set in Hoefler.

Written and illustrated by Marty Kelley. Art direction by Patrick Ready.

Kelley, Marty
    Summer Stinks / by Marty Kelley.
        p. cm.
    Summary: In this rhyming alphabet book, a boy lists all his reasons for disliking summer, from the ants that ate his snack to the zapper he touched by mistake.
    ISBN 1-55933-291-3
    [1. Summer –fiction. 2. Alphabet. 3. Stories in rhyme.] I. Title.
    PZ8.3.K298 Su 2001
    [E] –dc21

                                                                    2001017788
10 9 8 7 6 5 4 3 2

Summer Stinks

Lemonade
~~25¢~~ ~~50¢~~
~~10¢~~ free!

Words and pictures
by
Marty Kelley

Janell —
Hooray for bug spray!
Marty Kelley
2009

A is for Ants that ate my whole snack.

B   B is for Bug that crawled down my back.   **b**

C

C is for Castles the tide washed away.

C

D | D is for Dog-doo I stepped in today. | **d**

E E is Elastic that broke in my shorts. **e**

F

F is for Frog I found; he gave me warts.

f

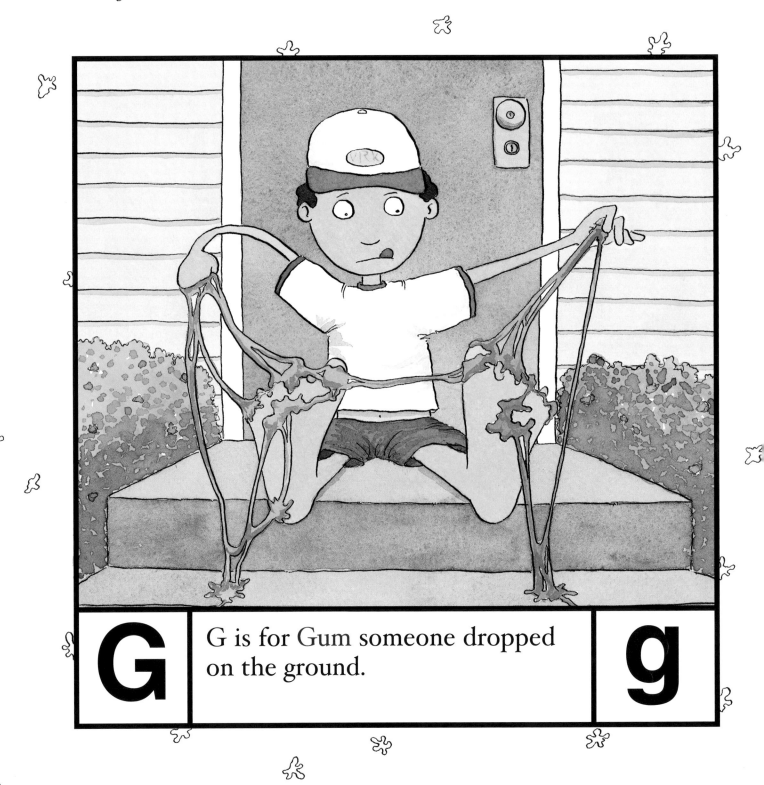

G   G is for Gum someone dropped on the ground.   **g**

H

H is for Heat stroke from running around.

h

I is for Ivy, the poisonous sort.

J J is for Jump rope that's one foot too short. **j**

K | K is for Kite that got stuck way up there. | **k**

L is for Lemonade; mine has a hair.

M M is Mosquitoes and Millions of bites.   **m**

N N is Not Sleeping on hot, sticky nights. **n**

O | O is for Ocean, as cold as can be. | O

P | P is for Popsicle, melting on me. | p

Q | Q is for Quicksand that's over my head. | **q**

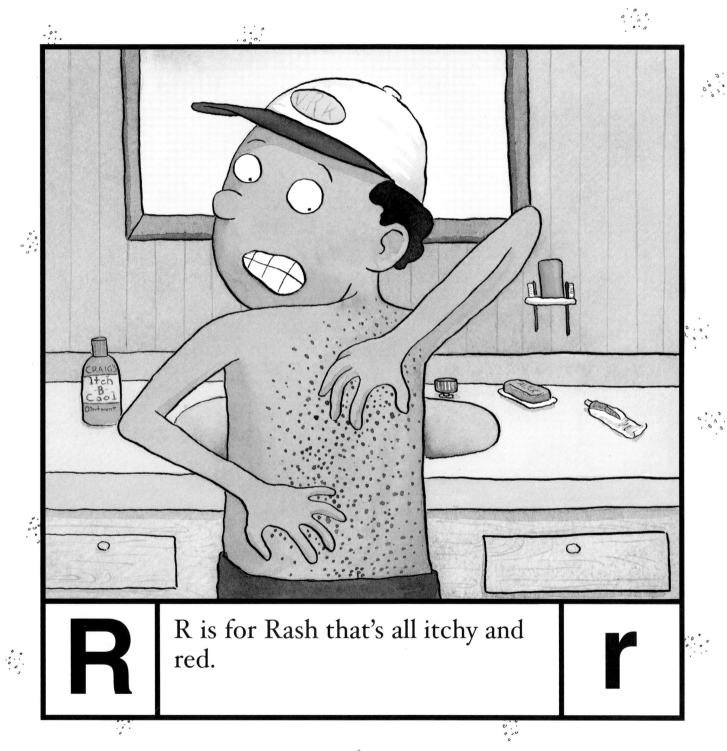

R | R is for Rash that's all itchy and red. | **r**

S

S is for Sunburn that's painful and pink.

S

T

T is for Thirsty; there's nothing to drink.

t

U

U is Umbrella that lets the rain through.

u

V V is Vacation with nothing to do. **V**

W W is Walking on sand that's too hot. **W**

X X marks the spot where the treasure is not. **X**

Y Y is my Yacht that just sank in the lake. **y**

Z Z is the Zapper I touched by mistake. **Z**

Twenty-six reasons this season's a bummer;
At least I can say there's no school in the summer.

The End

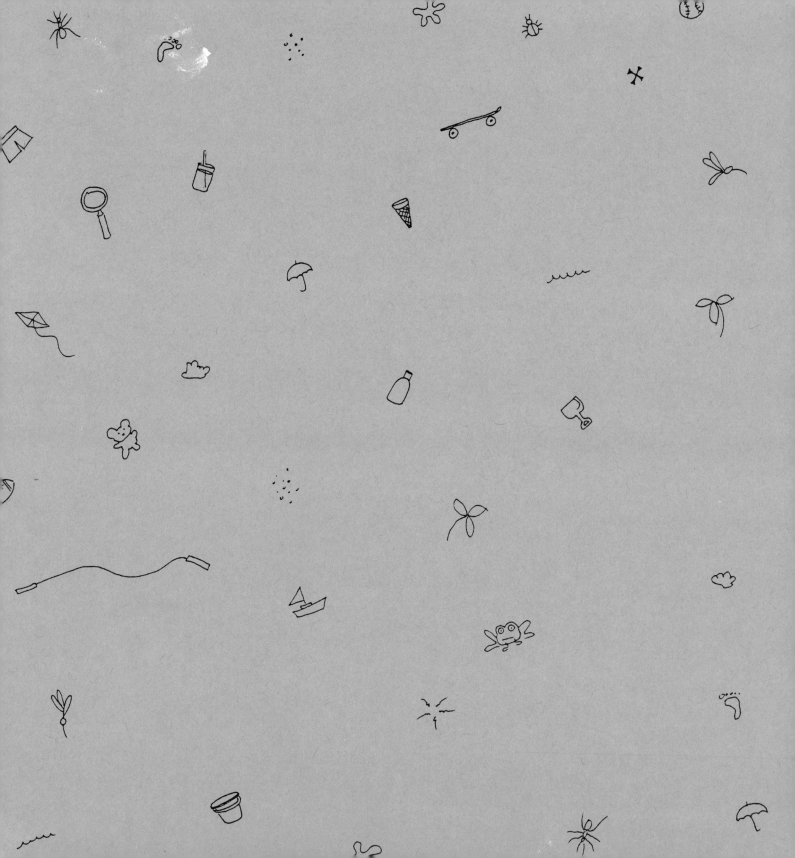